WHERE THINGS ARE
FROM NEAR TO FAR

By Tim Halbur and Chris Steins
Illustrated by David Ryan

PLANETIZEN PRESS

Where Things Are, From Near To Far

Published by Planetizen Press (www.planetizen.com), an imprint of Urban Insight, Inc.
All content and illustrations © 2008 by Urban Insight, Inc.
All rights reserved.
No part of this book may be reproduced in any form by any means without permission in
writing from the publisher.

Printed and bound in the United States of America.
First hardcover printing, 2008.

ISBN-978-0-9789329-2-3
Library of Congress Control Number: 2008910452

PLANETIZEN PRESS

Who's that frog, you may ask? Hugo's companion is a tribute to the very first kids book about
urban planning, *Neighbor Flap Foot, The City Planning Frog*, by Bill Ewald Jr. and Merle Henrickson,
published in 1952.

A Note on City Planning and the Transect

This book is based on the urban-to-rural transect, which divides cities into six different zones ranging from rural countryside to dense skyscrapers. The transect is a great way to look at the building blocks of a city, and to start thinking about how all the pieces of a city get planned in relation to one another. The urban transect was originally created by Andrés Duany, a Miami architect.

Every day, city planners help shape our cities and towns – making streets safe for pedestrians, fixing building designs so they meet the needs of citizens, improving traffic flow, creating bike paths and city parks, and preserving historic buildings. This book is a tribute to the work that they do in hopes that kids will learn more about this fascinating career at an early age.

Planetizen is an online resource for news and information, with daily news stories, features, job listings and opinion pieces exploring the world of city planning. You can find us at www.planetizen.com.

Hugo plays in the park,
with his favorite ball.

The park is in the city, where
buildings are REALLY TALL.

Hugo wonders,
"Who put these buildings here?
and what about that tree?"

"Who decides what goes where?"

His mom says, "Come with me..."

The city is full of shops and stores, and people everywhere!

People live above the stores, and bicycles ride by.

Houses, stores and offices
each have their separate place.

More cows than people live out here, and the bus runs out of stops.

Into the wilderness they go, where animals roam free.

The lake is home to ducks and fish,
and hives are full of bees.

"From the city to the country,
every building has its place."

Hugo's mother tells him,
with a smile upon her face.

"Who makes the city tall,

the suburbs wide,

and country wild?"

"That's my job," says Hugo's mom,
as she hugs her child.

"I'm an urban planner."

This book is dedicated to
Grant, Meera,
Rahul and Rowan,
and to the memory
of Susan Payne.